How Can I Touch the MOON

Cynthia McCalla

Illustrations: **Melyssa Proctor**

Balboa Press books may be ordered through booksellers or by contacting:

Balboa Press
A Division of Hay House
1663 Liberty Drive
Bloomington, IN 47403
www.balboapress.com
844-682-1282

Because of the dynamic nature of the Internet, any web addresses or
links contained in this book may have changed since publication and
may no longer be valid. The views expressed in this work are solely those
of the author and do not necessarily reflect the views of the publisher,
and the publisher hereby disclaims any responsibility for them.

Any people depicted in stock imagery provided by Getty Images are
models, and such images are being used for illustrative purposes only.
Certain stock imagery © Getty Images.

ISBN: 978-1-9822-6401-7 (sc)
978-1-9822-6402-4 (e)

Print information available on the last page.

Balboa Press rev. date: 02/13/2021

How Can I Touch the MOON

Outside, outside everybody outside!

Little Renny look, there's the moon.

Wow, Miss Dorothy it looks like I can almost touch it.

Miss Dorothy, how can I touch the moon?

If I stand on the slide and reach very high?

Oh, I wish I knew just how I can touch the moon.

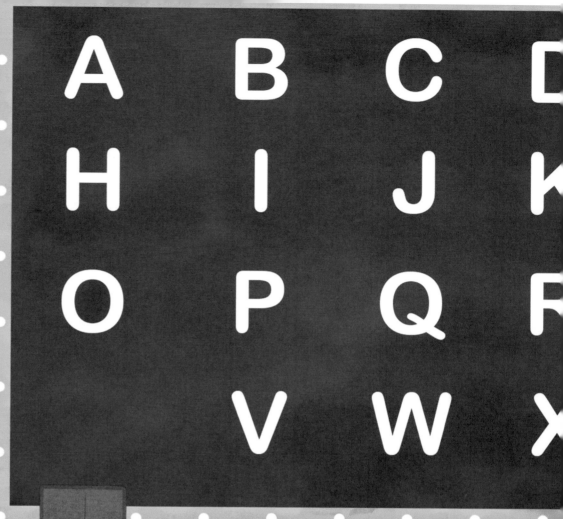

I know, maybe if I build a great big tower that can go through the roof and I climb on it, I could touch the moon.

How can I touch the moon daddy? Hi, Mr. Eli, did you get the water mommy left in the bag for you today? Mr. Eli, can you tell me how I can touch the moon.

Daddy can you lift me high high so I can touch the moon?

Good night Little Renny. Good night Daddy and Mommy. Mommy, can you tell me how I can touch the moon?

Pola, look outside, It's getting so dark.
Look at the moon, it's so big and bright.

Maybe if I close my eyes so very very very tight…(snoring) Look Little Renny has fallen asleep. What is he dreaming about?

Weeeee Pola we are on our way.

Oh, oh, what happened to our ride? Look like we have to catch a ride on something else Pola, but what?

I know a rocket ship. It will take us right to the moon.
Pola look, we are almost there.

Miss Dorothy, Miss Dorothy…

Guess where I went last night?

I touched the moon.

Printed in the United States
By Bookmasters